Mr Croc was late.

He was supposed to be at the cinema.

His friend, Mr Hound, was waiting
for him outside.

'I stayed in bed too long,' Mr Croc
panted, mopping his brow.

Rockets

MR CROC

Mr Croc's Clock

Frank Rodgers

A & C Black • London

Rockets

MR CROC - Frank Rodgers

What Mr Croc Forgot
Mr Croc's Clock
Mr Croc's Walk
Mr Croc's Silly Sock

First paperback edition 1999
First published 1999 in hardback by
A & C Black (Publishers) Ltd
35 Bedford Row, London WC1R 4JH

ISBN 0-7136-5046-X

A CIP catalogue record for this book is available
from the British Library.

Printed and bound by G. Z. Printek, Bilbao, Spain.

'You need an alarm clock,' replied
Mr Hound.
'You're right,' agreed Mr Croc.

Mr Croc enjoyed the film.
The hero grinned a lot...

...and performed amazing stunts.

Aha!

'His smile is almost as nice as mine,' thought Mr Croc.

I wonder if I could be like him?

As they came out of the cinema,
Mr Croc smiled his lovely smile.

'Yes, I have, haven't I?' said Mr Croc.
He smiled even more – showing all of his
one hundred teeth.

'But even film stars have to get up
in the morning,' said Mr Hound.

Mr Croc was very forgetful.

They hurried off to the jeweller's shop.

Mr Croc bought a big alarm clock from Mrs Spring.

'This will certainly wake you up in the morning,' said Mrs Spring.

'Wonderful!' said Mr Croc.

Mr Hound and Mr Croc headed home.
'Let's go to the cinema again tomorrow,'
said Mr Hound.

That night, Mr Croc set the alarm before
going to bed.

He snuggled down and was soon fast
asleep. Mr Croc dreamed he was a film
star with big muscles and flashing teeth.

He dreamed he could do amazing stunts...
swinging from tree to tree...

...and leaping
over buses.

Then Mr Croc dreamed he was climbing a huge clock tower...

...when suddenly...

...it struck one and he fell off.

Mr Croc managed to catch hold
of the clock's little hand...

...when...

...the clock struck two.

Mr Croc nearly fell off again.

'Help!' he cried.

But the clock hadn't finished.

It struck three and Mr Croc wobbled.

It struck four and Mr Croc fell off...

...and woke up.

Mr Croc was very confused. Then he realised – it wasn't the clock in his dream that had gone BONG!
It was his alarm clock.

You were supposed to go RRIIING!

BONG!

It was still very early, but Mr Croc
decided to get up.

But the clock had other ideas. Every time
Mr Croc started to make his breakfast the
clock went BONG!

BONG!

Mr Croc burnt the toast.

BONG!

He forgot to stir his porridge.

BONG!

He dropped all the eggs.

'Oh dear,' said Mr Croc.

I'll have to take you back to the shop.

He put the clock into his bag and set off.
His tummy rumbled as he walked along.

At the shops he met Mr Hound.

Hello, Mr Croc. You're early!

Am I? What am I early for?

Just then Mr Croc's tummy rumbled loudly.

'I'm hungry,' he said. 'I haven't had any breakfast.'

'Let's go to the cafe,' said Mr Hound.

Mr Hound ordered a cup of tea.
Mr Croc ordered egg and chips with
extra chips and eggs.

But just as the waitress was about to
place it on the table...

BONG!

'Aaah!' cried the waitress and jumped in fright.

The plate went flying.

Mr Hound caught it...

... but the food went everywhere.

BONG! went the clock again.
The waitress was not amused. 'Take that
silly bonging thing out of this cafe!'

Mr Hound and Mr Croc hurried outside. 'Now I remember why I came to the shops,' said Mr Croc. 'I wanted to get my clock fixed.'

Mrs Poodle was walking by.
She got such a fright she dropped
her pot plant.

Mr Hound caught it just in time.

Mr Croc took the clock out of his bag.

Outside the cinema they saw Mr Flicks, the owner.

'I'm trying to shoo away these pigeons,' replied Mr Flicks.

'I know,' sighed Mr Flicks.

Mr Flicks looked at his watch. 'The film is about to start,' he said. 'You'd better hurry.'

Mr Croc and Mr Hound dashed into the cinema.

Mr Croc was so hungry that he bought a big bag of popcorn.

But just as they sat down the clock went BONG!

Mr Croc's tummy rumbled.

Then the film started and he soon forgot about being hungry.

The handsome hero, special agent number seven, had a flashy smile.

Mr Croc watched as the special hero did some amazing stunts...

...and then began to chat to a beautiful lady.

'Hello,' said the special agent, smiling his flashy smile.

The whole audience burst out laughing.

The audience laughed even more.
Mr Croc's face went very red.

The usherette shone her torch on him.

'Oh dear,' said Mr Croc.

As they came outside, the clock
let out another loud

'COOO!' cried the
pigeons and
flew off in alarm.

'Ahh!' cried Mr Flicks
and wobbled
on his ladder.

40

Mr Hound held it steady.

'My alarm clock,' said Mr Croc.

'It won't stop going BONG!'

'No, it's wonderful!' said Mr Flicks.

Mr Croc smiled.

'But I must give you something in return,' said Mr Flicks.

Mr Croc's tummy rumbled.

'Some popcorn would be nice,' he said.

'Of course!' said Mr Flicks and fetched a huge bag.

'Anything else?' asked Mr Flicks.

Mr Croc shook his head but Mr Hound smiled.

Mr Flicks thought for a moment.
'I've got an idea!' He fetched a video
camera and pointed it at Mr Croc.

Then Mr Croc held up the clock and
said a few words to the camera.

Next day Mr Croc and Mr Hound were back at the cinema in the front row. Mr Croc was very excited.

The lights went down and the curtains opened.

TA-RAAA!

went the music... and a notice appeared on the screen.

MR FLICKS WOULD
LIKE TO THANK
MR CROC FOR HIS
KIND GIFT.

Mr Croc beamed.

Then suddenly, there was Mr Croc himself, smiling his lovely smile up on the big screen.

BONG!

went the clock and Mr Croc smiled even more.

'It's time for the film!' he said.

The audience cheered and Mr Hound
clapped his hands.

Mr Croc smiled his lovely smile.
'Thanks to you, Mr Hound,' he said.

The End